ALICE McLERRAN

ROXABOXEN

ILLUSTRATED BY

BARBARA COONEY

SCHOLASTIC INC.

New York   Toronto   London   Auckland   Sydney

ISBN 0-590-45589-3

Text copyright © 1991 by Alice McLerran.
Illustrations copyright © 1991 by Barbara Cooney.
Originally published by William Morrow & Company, Inc.
All rights reserved. Published by Scholastic Inc.,
730 Broadway, New York, NY 10003, by arrangement with
Puffin Books, a division of Penguin Books USA Inc.,
375 Hudson St., New York, New York 10014.
12 11 10 9 8 7 6 5 4 3 2 1   2 3 4 5 6 7/9

Printed in the U.S.A.   08
First Scholastic printing, October 1992

ROXABOXEN

To May Cargill Doan and all her line   —A.M.

For my Roxaboxen guide, Tahe   —B.C.

Marian called it Roxaboxen.
(She always knew the name of everything.)
There across the road, it looked like any rocky hill—
nothing but sand and rocks, some old wooden boxes,
cactus and greasewood and thorny ocotillo—
but it was a special place.

The street between Roxaboxen and the houses curved like a river,
so Marian named it the River Rhode.
After that you had to ford a river to reach Roxaboxen.

Of course all of Marian's sisters came:
Anna May and Frances and little Jean.
Charles from next door, even though he was twelve.
Oh, and Eleanor, naturally,
and Jamie with his brother Paul.
Later on there were others, but these were the first.

Well, not really the first.
Roxaboxen had always been there
and must have belonged to others, long before.

When Marian dug up a tin box filled with round black pebbles
everyone knew what it was:
it was a buried treasure.
Those pebbles were the money of Roxaboxen.
You could still find others like them if you looked hard enough.
So some days became treasure-hunting days, with everybody trying to
    find that special kind.
And then on other days you might just find one without even looking.

A town of Roxaboxen began to grow, traced in lines of stone:

Main Street first, edged with the whitest ones,

and then the houses.

Charles made his of the biggest stones.

After all, he was the oldest.

At first the houses were very plain, but soon they all began to

add more rooms.

The old wooden boxes could be shelves or tables or anything you wanted.

You could find pieces of pottery for dishes.

Round pieces were best.

Later on there was a town hall.
Marian was mayor, of course;
that was just the way she was.
Nobody minded.

After a while they added other streets.
Frances moved to one of them and built herself a new house outlined
   in desert glass,
bits of amber, amethyst, and sea-green:
a house of jewels.